Princesses Don't Wear Jeans

**Other Shooting Star books
you may enjoy:**

Princesses Don't Wear Jeans

Brenda Bellingham

illustrations by Carol Wakefield

Scholastic Canada Ltd.

Canadian Cataloguing in Publication Data

Bellingham, Brenda, 1931-
    Princesses don't wear jeans

(Shooting star)
ISBN 0-590-73766-X

I. Wakefield, Carol. II. Title. III. Series

PS8553.E468P7 1991   jC813'.54   C90-095872-3
PZ7.B45Pr 1991

8 7 6 5 4   Printed in Canada   3 4 5 6 7/9
                    Manufactured by Webcom Limited

Contents

Chapter 1

Wild Bears

Jeff Brown's real name was Justinian Edwin Frederick Fotheringham Brown.

"When you have a name like Brown, you have to fancy it up," said Mr. Brown, Jeff's dad. "Otherwise people get you mixed up with all the other Browns around."

Jeff did not mind being a Brown. Brown was just right for him. His hair was shiny brown and his eyes were shiny brown. In the summer his skin turned a healthy brown colour. Brown was a plain, ordinary name. It suited Jeff just fine.

Justinian Edwin Frederick Fotheringham did

not suit him. It was too different. Jeff did not want to be different. He wanted to be like everybody else. When people asked him his name, he said, "My name is Jeff." He made this up from his initials. "I'm Jeff Brown," he said.

Mr. and Mrs. Brown loved their son. When they saw that Jeff did not like his fancy name they did not argue. They called him Jeff.

One day a new girl came to Jeff's school. The principal brought her to the grade three room.

"This is Matilda Perkins," the principal said. "She likes to be called Tilly."

"Welcome to our class, Tilly," said Mrs. Frank, Jeff's teacher.

Tilly Perkins stood at the front of the room. She wore tights that were too big. They twisted around her skinny legs like two corkscrews. She wore a skirt that was too long. The hem went up and down like a roller coaster. Her sweater had a hole in the elbow. She had forgotten to brush her hair. All the grade three kids stared at her.

Jeff knew he would not feel good if a bunch of kids stared at him.

"Hi, Tilly," he said.

Poppy Rose sat behind Jeff. She poked him in the back with her fingers. He knew what she meant. She meant, Don't be nice to that new kid, or else. Poppy Rose glared at Tilly.

Did Tilly Perkins quake?

Did Tilly Perkins quiver?

No, she did not. She looked around in a friendly way. She had hazel eyes that were bright and twinkly.

Mrs. Frank smiled at Jeff. "Tilly, you can sit in the desk next to Jeff," she said. Tilly Perkins went to her desk with a hop, skip and a jump. She beamed at Jeff.

Tilly Perkins is a very brave girl, thought Jeff.

Everyone in the grade three class kept a journal. Each day they all had to write some news in it. It was like keeping a diary. Some of the kids liked to read what they wrote out loud.

Jeff wished they wouldn't. Mostly what they wrote was boring. Sally's news was that her grandma was coming to stay. What kind of news is that, wondered Jeff. Sally's grandma was always coming to stay. Bruno's family had bought a new TV. Bruno's family was always buying something new. Tilly listened politely to the other children.

"Is there anybody else?" Mrs. Frank asked.

Tilly put up her hand. "Last night I played with my wild bears," she read. "I have two of them. Their names are Chum and Champ. We went down to the river and swam and Chum caught some fish."

The kids stared at her. Their mouths fell open with surprise.

Jeff smiled. Tilly Perkins had two wild bears. Now *that* was news.

"Tilly, I don't think you understand," said Mrs. Frank. "We write only true things in our journals. Later on we'll write stories."

"Please, Teacher, it is true," said Tilly.

"Tilly, I like to be called Mrs. Frank, not Teacher," said Mrs. Frank. "Don't you mean you played with your teddy bears?"

"No, Mrs. Frank," Tilly said. "These are wild bears."

A lot of people giggled. Poppy Rose said loudly, "Prove it. Bring them to school."

Did Tilly Perkins stammer?

Did Tilly Perkins stutter?

No, she did not. Tilly looked Mrs. Frank straight in the eye. "Please, Teacher, can I bring them to school?"

Mrs. Frank sighed. "As long as you keep them on good strong chains," she said.

Tilly Perkins is not an ordinary girl, thought Jeff. She is different. He could hardly wait for Tilly Perkins to bring her wild bears to school.

Chapter 2

Princess Matilda

At recess Tilly asked Mrs. Frank for a ball to take outside. "Come on," she called. "Who wants to play ball?" Tilly didn't wait to put on a jacket. She got to the playground first.

Jeff and Bruno were second. "Where's the ball?" Jeff asked.

Tilly pointed to the sky. "Up there," she said. Jeff looked up. High up in the blue sky he saw a pale, round shape.

"That's the moon," said Bruno scornfully. "I want the ball. Where is it?"

Bruno lived next door to Jeff. He was a tough

kid. Nobody ever argued with Bruno.

Did Tilly Perkins shake?

Did Tilly Perkins shiver?

No, she did not. Tilly Perkins argued.

"That's not the moon," she said. "The moon doesn't shine in the daytime." She pointed proudly at the pale round shape in the sky. "I kicked the ball so high it stuck up there."

"You're crazy," Bruno said.

Jeff gazed up at the moon. It looked just like the white ball Mrs. Frank had given Tilly. He chuckled. Tilly Perkins had legs like sticks. No one with legs like sticks could kick a ball that far. Tilly Perkins had a good imagination.

Poppy Rose and Sally Topp came out. Sally lived on Jeff's street. Poppy was her best friend.

"Your hem is falling down," Poppy told Tilly.

Did Tilly Perkins blush?

Did Tilly Perkins blubber?

No, she did not. Tilly looked down. "Yes, it is," she said.

"You should ask your mother to sew it up," Sally said.

"She hasn't got time," Tilly answered. "She has to look after all our wild animals."

"I bet," said Poppy.

"Where do you live?" Sally asked.

"On a farm," said Tilly. "It's a wild animal farm."

Poppy looked at Sally. They giggled. "Why don't you wear jeans, then?"

Tilly held up her chin. "Because I'm going to be a princess when I grow up," she said. "Princesses don't wear jeans."

Most of the grade three class had gathered around. They nudged one another and laughed. "Princess Matilda!"

"Some princess," Poppy said. "Your sweater has a hole in it and it smells."

Did Tilly Perkins cry?

Did Tilly Perkins cringe?

No, she didn't. Tilly Perkins held her arm close to her nose. She sniffed, long and lovingly. "Yes," she said. "It does. It smells of wild bear. I wore it when I fed them. I expect they made the hole with their sharp claws."

Tilly Perkins is not a vain girl, thought Jeff.

"Come on, you guys," Tilly cried, "let's climb the monkey bars. Race you, Jeff."

"*You* climb the monkey bars," said Bruno. "I found the ball. It was in the bushes. We're going to play soccer. Come on, Jeff. You're on my team."

The other kids ran after Bruno. Jeff did not know what to do. He wanted to find out more about the wild bears. But if he went with Tilly, Bruno would get mad. So would Poppy and Sally.

Nick and Alex, the twins, followed Tilly. Bruno didn't care if they went. They were no good at soccer.

Jeff decided. He ran after Bruno.

The next morning Jeff watched for Tilly. He wondered if she would bring her wild bears to school. He saw her get off the school bus. No bears got off with her.

"Why didn't you bring the wild bears?" he asked her.

"My mother wouldn't let me," she said.

"Liar, liar, pants on fire!" said Poppy.

"I'll try to bring them tomorrow," said Tilly.

She didn't. But every day she wrote in her journal about the bears.

Tuesday: The wild bears played in their bathtub, she wrote. Champ swallowed the soap. He blew soap bubbles.

Wednesday: The wild bears played Frisbee with an old car tire. The tire fell over Chum's head. She wore it like a hula hoop.

Thursday: My wild bears are very strong. They like to wrestle. Usually Champ wins. That's why I call him Champ.

Jeff longed to see the bears. Every day he asked Tilly to bring them to school. Every day she said she would.

"You can't bring wild bears to school," Bruno said scornfully. "They'd tear everybody apart."

"These are still babies," Tilly said. "They're cubs. I'll bring them tomorrow."

But she didn't. The other kids left her alone. They didn't play with her.

"She tells lies," Poppy said.

"She's crazy," Bruno added. "If you believe she's got wild bears, you're crazy too," he told Jeff.

Jeff stopped asking Tilly about the bears. He wished Tilly would stop writing stories about them. He wished she would wear jeans instead of twisty tights. He wished she would get her mother to mend her hem and wash her sweater. Maybe then the other kids would like her. He still liked Tilly, even if she did make up stories.

Then one day Tilly came late to school. Eyes shining, she bounded into the classroom. "Teacher, I brought my wild bears," she said. "They're outside. Should I bring them in?"

Mrs. Frank looked nervous. "Yes, Tilly," she said. "I suppose you should."

Tilly came back into the room with a bear under each arm. Each bear had a chain around its neck. Each bear was on a leash. Tilly stood them on the floor. Their legs stuck out stiffly. Their brown eyes stared glassily at the grade threes.

The grade threes stared back at the bears.

Chapter 3

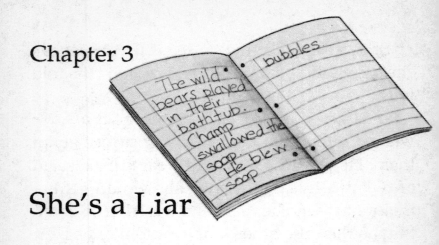

She's a Liar

"This is Chum and this is Champ," said Tilly. Her eyes sparkled.

The wild bears didn't move. They were stuffed toys!

Tilly Perkins likes to tease, thought Jeff.

The other kids began to talk all at the same time. They had been excited when Tilly said she'd brought the bears. Now they were disappointed. They were mad at Tilly.

"I told you she tells lies," Poppy said.

"Poppy, that's not nice," said Mrs. Frank.

Did Tilly Perkins cry?

Did Tilly Perkins confess?

No, she did not. Tilly Perkins chuckled. "These are *pretend* wild bears," she said.

"Tilly, sit down now," said Mrs. Frank. "You and I will talk later."

"See!" Bruno said to Jeff. "I told you Tilly Perkins was crazy."

"She's not crazy," Jeff said. "She was joking. Anyway, her bears *aren't* teddy bears. They look just like wild bears."

"So?" said Bruno. "Maybe you're crazy too. Maybe I shouldn't play soccer with you."

"You don't have to," Jeff said. "I don't care."

But he did care. He did not talk to Tilly Perkins any more. Nick and Alex were the only ones who played with her. And who wanted to play with guys who couldn't kick a ball?

Tilly did. At recess she pretended there was a bear cave under the bushes. She and the twins and the bears lived there. Great growls came from the cave. Excited squeals came from the cave. Laughter and giggles came from there,

too. Jeff wondered if Tilly Perkins was really having fun. Maybe she was only pretending.

After Mrs. Frank talked to her, Tilly Perkins did not tell any more news about her bears. Jeff missed Tilly's news. Now the news was boring —like stuff about Sally's grandma. Jeff yawned. It was hard to listen politely.

Did Tilly Perkins frown?

Did Tilly Perkins fidget?

No, she did not. Tilly Perkins wrote pages and pages in her journal. Mrs. Frank pretended not to notice.

"What's she writing?" Poppy whispered in Jeff's ear. Jeff wondered if Tilly was writing about her bears. He leaned over to see. He leaned over so far he fell off his chair. His cheeks were hot.

"Did you see?" whispered Poppy.

"No," Jeff said.

He didn't try to see Tilly's journal again. Maybe now that Tilly had stopped talking about her wild bears the other kids would forget them. If Tilly Perkins stopped telling stories, maybe the other kids would get to like her and start to play with her. Jeff sure hoped so.

Chapter 4

Tilly's Dragon

The grade threes were studying pioneers. Mrs. Frank gave out large pieces of card.

"Today you can make pioneer homesteads," said Mrs. Frank. "Some of you can make a log cabin in the woods. Some can make a house of sods on the prairie. Work in pairs. Jeff, you work with Tilly."

Bruno scowled. He wanted Jeff to be his partner.

"I can't help it," Jeff whispered to Bruno. "Mrs. Frank says I have to work with Tilly Perkins." But he didn't really mind.

Jeff drew a big river right across the card. Pioneers liked to be near water. He and Tilly painted the river blue and the rest of the card green.

"Let's make a log cabin," Jeff said.

"Okay," said Tilly.

Jeff got started. Tilly went to the scrap box and found a paper bag. She stuffed it with newspaper and crumpled it. She got some tape and stuck the crumpled bag on the card.

"What's that?" Jeff asked.

"It's a mountain," Tilly said.

That's okay, thought Jeff. Some pioneers might have lived near the mountains.

Tilly painted the mountain green and brown. The green and brown paint ran. The mountain looked dark and dismal. Jeff built his log cabin on the opposite side of the river from the mountain.

Tilly got some brown construction paper from the scrap box. Jeff thought she was going to make logs. Instead she made a tall, square tower. She cut out some squares around the top.

"What's that?" Jeff asked.

"A castle," said Tilly.

"Pioneers didn't live in castles," Jeff said. "Castles are for knights in armour and stuff like that." Tilly Perkins hadn't been at school when they started doing pioneers. Maybe she didn't know.

"The castle isn't for your pioneers," Tilly said. "It's for my dragon. I have one at home. He likes to sleep in a dark dungeon. Sometimes he sunbathes in the courtyard. At night, when no one's looking, he flies around the towers."

"If no one's looking, how do you know he flies around?" Jeff asked.

"He told me," Tilly said.

She stuck the castle on top of the paper bag mountain. The castle looked as if it might tumble down the mountain at any minute. It was just the sort of place where a dragon might lurk. A castle is a lot more fun than a pioneer cabin, thought Jeff.

Bruno walked over and looked at Jeff and Tilly's work. "I'm telling," he said. "Mrs. Frank said to make a pioneer homestead. Pioneers didn't live in castles."

"Some of them did," Tilly said.

"No, they didn't," Jeff said. "They didn't have time. They were always tilling and sowing and reaping."

He felt sorry for the pioneers. All they did was work. Mrs. Frank said they had fun too. She said they had barn raising bees and quilting bees. To Jeff it sounded like another name for work. Pioneers lived hard lives in the new land. Jeff wondered why they'd bothered to come.

"I know," he said. "The dragon's castle is on the other side of the ocean. The dragon scared the pioneers. That's why they came here."

"Where's the ocean?" asked Bruno.

Jeff pointed to the part he had painted blue.

"It looks like a river," said Bruno.

"Well, it isn't," said Jeff. "It's the ocean. This side is the old country. That's where the dragon is. This side is the new country. That's where the pioneer cabin is."

Mrs. Frank came to see what the arguing was

about. She cut the card in half and told Jeff to finish his homestead on his half. She gave Tilly a new piece of card and made her start again.

Did Tilly Perkins sob?

Did Tilly Perkins sigh?

No, she did not. "Please, Teacher, can I take the castle home for my dragon?" she asked.

"Tilly Perkins says she has a dragon at home," said Poppy.

Everybody laughed.

"Why don't you bring it to school?" asked Sally in a teasing voice.

"Dragons aren't like dogs," said Tilly Perkins. "You can't take them around on a leash. Dragons are reptiles. They're cold-blooded."

That sounds right, thought Jeff. Tilly Perkins tells good stories. If only she wouldn't pretend they're true.

"Sure," said Bruno, grinning. "And dragons catch people. Her dragon would eat up everybody in this room."

He made growling noises and made his hands look like claws. Then he laughed like a donkey.

Did Tilly Perkins flinch?

Did Tilly Perkins fume?

No, she did not. "I can bring a picture of my dragon to school," she said.

Jeff sighed. A picture wouldn't prove anything. You could find dragon pictures in lots of places. The other kids never would like Tilly. How could he ever be her friend?

Chapter 5

Bruno
Poppy
Sally
Todd
Michael
John
Lauren
Tanya
Emily
Robin

Some Party

This time Jeff didn't get impatient. He didn't want Tilly to bring her dragon picture. He knew the other kids would laugh at her. He hoped she'd forget about it.

"I brought the picture of my dragon," Tilly said, a few days later.

"Who cares?" said Bruno.

"We all know what dragons look like," said Poppy.

"They're in lots of books," said Sally.

Jeff felt sorry for Tilly. "Let *me* see," he said. He looked over Tilly's shoulder.

This isn't a book picture, he thought. It isn't from a calendar. It isn't a painting at all. He felt a little thrill of excitement. Maybe the dragon was true after all.

Tilly pointed. "There's my dragon. He's in his lair."

The dragon was partly in the shadows. Jeff took the picture from Tilly. He wanted to see it better.

"What's she talking about?" asked Bruno. He pushed between Jeff and Tilly.

Poppy and Sally crowded behind Jeff and looked over his shoulders.

"Looks like a dinosaur," said Bruno.

Jeff looked hard at the creature in the picture. It *could* be a dinosaur. Some dinosaurs weren't all that big. "You can buy postcards with dinosaur pictures," said Sally. "I bet she got it at the museum."

Jeff peered at Tilly's picture. "This thing's got scales like a dragon," he said. "And it's green. It has a long tail that comes to a point. And the scales go in rings around its tail. And it has five

toes on each foot. It *could* be a dragon."

"It's not a dragon," said Poppy, firmly. "Dragons have zig zag things down their backs."

"This one's got things down its back," said Jeff.

"They're not dragon things," said Sally. "They're like the teeth on a comb."

Jeff turned the picture over. "This isn't a postcard," he said. "It's a photo."

"That's right, Jeff," said Tilly. "My dad took it."

"Huh!" said Poppy. "I bet you made it out of Plasticine. I saw on TV how they make horror movies. They make models and take close-ups. They look just like the real thing."

"This looks like a real live animal," said Jeff.

"Don't be crazy," said Bruno. "There's no such thing as a dragon. Come on. Let's play soccer."

"Yeah," said Sally. "We've got better things to do than look at dumb pictures."

"You can't believe a word that girl says," said

Poppy. "My mother says I shouldn't even talk to people like her."

Bruno, Poppy and Sally went away in disgust.

Jeff looked at the picture a bit longer. He really wanted to believe Tilly Perkins. He had to be quite sure he was right.

"I know what this is a photo of," he said at last.

"A dragon," said Tilly.

"No," said Jeff. "An iguana. They had one in the children's library near where I used to live."

"Come on, Jeff," yelled Bruno. "Stop talking to that dumb kid."

"If you talk to her, we're not talking to you," called Poppy.

Jeff gave the photo back to Tilly Perkins. "You shouldn't make things up, Tilly Perkins," he said. "How do you expect people to like you?"

He walked away sadly. He didn't feel like playing soccer. But he didn't feel like talking to Tilly Perkins any more either.

Jeff's birthday was coming. In two weeks he would be nine years old. He always had a party on his birthday. That evening, his mom and dad talked about it.

"Make a list of the kids you want to invite," Mom said. "I'll buy the invitations."

Jeff sat at the table and chewed his pencil.

"First put down the names of your best friends," Dad said. "Then add all the kids who invited you to their parties."

Pretty soon Jeff had a very long list. Dad looked at it and laughed.

"Twenty-one kids," he said. "How many kids are in your room?"

"Twenty-four," Jeff said.

"That's too many," Mom said. "Choose ten."

"I can't," Jeff said. "The kids who get left out feel bad."

"We can have a big party," Dad said. "We can go to the park and have a picnic. But what about the three kids you left out?"

"Nick and Alex can't kick a ball," Jeff said. "They can't even catch a ball. No one wants to play with them. And Tilly Perkins makes things up."

"What sort of things?" asked Mom.

"She said she had wild bears at home. She brought them to school. They were only stuffed toys. She says she has a dragon at home. There's no such thing. Mrs. Frank says dragons are mythical beasts. Tilly Perkins brought a photo to school. She said it was her dragon. I know what it was. It was an iguana."

"An iguana!" said Jeff's dad. "That's an unusual pet."

Jeff hadn't thought that the iguana might be Tilly's pet. "It might not be hers," he said. "With Tilly Perkins you just never know."

Jeff's mom smiled. "Tilly Perkins sounds like fun," she said. "She must have a good imagination."

"Well, no one wants to play with her," Jeff said.

"You can't leave out just three kids," his Dad answered.

Jeff felt sick. He knew what Poppy and Sally and Bruno would say. "Maybe I won't have a party this year," he said.

"Jeff," his dad said firmly. "Do what you know is right."

When Dad spoke like that it was no use arguing. "Okay," Jeff said, with a sigh. "I'll ask everybody."

Mom hugged him. "That's our boy," she said. "Your father and I are proud of you."

This time Mom's hug did not make Jeff feel better. If he invited Tilly Perkins, Bruno wouldn't come. Poppy wouldn't come either, or Sally. The other kids always copied Bruno and Poppy and Sally. So no one would come. Tilly Perkins and the twins would be the only ones at his party.

Some party!

Chapter 6

White Mice

At school Jeff gave out his party invitations. He left the twins and Tilly until last. Maybe he could give them their invitations when no one else was looking, he thought. But sharp-eyed Poppy spied the three invitations in his desk.

"You forgot some," she said. "Come on. I'll help you give them out."

"No!" cried Jeff. "I can do it."

He was too late. Poppy had already grabbed the invitations.

"You're inviting Nick and Alex?" she said, wrinkling her nose. "Yech!"

"My dad said I had to," Jeff said. His cheeks felt hot.

"Poor kid!" Poppy looked sorry for Jeff. "Who's the other one for?" She looked at the last envelope. There was no name written on it.

"Never mind," Jeff said.

Then he saw Tilly watching him. Her eyes were bright and hopeful. When she saw him look at her she turned away.

Jeff knew how he would feel if he were the only one who got left out of a party. "Tilly," he called after her. "This is for you." He tried to smile. Maybe she can't come, he thought.

Tilly read her invitation. A grin spread over her face. The twinkle came back into her eyes.

"Thanks, Jeff," she said. "I love parties."

Poppy stuck her nose in the air. "I don't think I can make it," she said. "My mother won't let me go around with liars."

"Mine neither," said Sally.

"What did you want to ask *her* for?" Bruno asked Jeff. "Are you crazy, or something?"

"He asked the twins too," Sally said.

"I'm not going to any party with a bunch of crazies," Bruno said.

Did Tilly Perkins mope?

Did Tilly Perkins mind?

No, she did not. Tilly Perkins grinned at Jeff. "Jeff, I'm going to give you a great birthday present," she said.

"Yeah!" Bruno sneered. "A couple of wild bears!"

"No," said Poppy. "A dragon."

Everybody laughed. Everybody except Tilly and Jeff. Jeff didn't care what kind of gift Tilly gave him. It didn't matter. He just wished Tilly wouldn't make things up. He wished she'd try to be more like the other kids. Then he could be her friend.

"Do you like white mice, Jeff?" Tilly asked.

"Sure," Jeff said. He wasn't sure. He'd never seen white mice.

"I've got lots. I've got a Mouse Town at home. I'll give you some for your birthday," Tilly said.

Jeff hoped she wouldn't. He didn't think his mother would care for mice, white or not.

"Oh sure!" Bruno said, disgusted. "Cute little stuffed mice. Just what Jeff always wanted."

"You must get a cage for them," Tilly said, ignoring Bruno. "And a little wheel to run around on. They need exercise."

For once, Bruno looked unsure of himself. "Maybe I *will* come to your party, Jeff. I'd better come and check out those white mice."

"Me too," said Poppy. "I bet Tilly Perkins is lying again."

Jeff wasn't sure if he should believe Tilly Perkins. He'd better tell his parents about the mice. Just in case.

He mentioned it at supper that night.

"Tilly Perkins might give me some mice for my birthday," he said. "Is that okay?"

"Mice!" Jeff's mom cried. "What kind of mice?"

"White mice," Jeff said.

"When I was a boy I knew a kid who kept white mice," Dad said. "They make good pets."

"Okay, Jeff," said Mom. "As long as you keep them in your own room. And look after them yourself. And don't let them escape. We don't want the house overrun with mice."

Jeff wondered what to do. Should he get a mouse cage? What if Tilly brought stuffed mice, like Bruno said? A mouse cage would be a waste of money. And the other kids would laugh at him. They'd say he was crazy to believe Tilly Perkins.

But what if Tilly brought real live white mice? He wouldn't have a cage for them. Tilly would know he had not believed her. He didn't want to hurt Tilly's feelings. Whatever he did, things would not turn out right.

One way or another, his ninth birthday was going to be a total disaster.

Chapter 7

Tilly Perkins is Worth It

At school Tilly talked about her mice.

"In Mouse Town, the mice live in apartments," she said. "They have roads with bridges and tunnels."

"Sure," said Bruno, grinning. "And they drive around in Jeeps."

Tilly looked interested.

"That's a good idea," she said. "I should buy them some cars to ride in."

Poppy and Sally grinned too.

"They must have a pretty big cage," said Poppy.

"As big as a house," said Sally.

"It's big, all right," said Tilly. "And the walls are made of glass. I can see everything that happens in Mouse Town."

Tilly's Mouse Town sounds like fun, thought Jeff. "I could buy an aquarium for my mice," he said. "Then I could see what they do."

"You must be out of your mind," said Bruno. "Aquariums cost big bucks."

"She'll never bring the mice," said Poppy.

"And you'll have wasted your allowance," said Sally.

"What about that model airplane you're saving up for?" asked Bruno. "The one you can fly. A plane's better than any dumb aquarium."

"A person would be crazy to believe anything Tilly Perkins says," said Poppy.

Did Tilly Perkins look wan?

Did Tilly Perkins look worried?

No, she did not. Tilly Perkins smiled. Her

hazel eyes twinkled. "Jeff believes me," she said.

Tilly Perkins trusts me, thought Jeff. He couldn't let her down. He'd have to buy a mouse cage. He could put off the airplane for a while.

"I have to buy a cage for Tilly Perkins's mice," he told his dad. "Can I use the money I've been saving?"

"If you want to," said his dad. "It's your money." His dad took him along to the pet shop. They looked around.

Jeff stopped in front of a big glass case. "Those are iguanas," he said to his dad. "They look kind of like dragons, don't they?"

Dad chuckled. "They sure do."

The clerk saw them looking. "Iguanas can grow to be five feet long, plus a tail," he said.

"I vote we stick to mice," said his dad.

No wonder Tilly said she couldn't bring her dragon to school, thought Jeff.

"How much is that mouse cage?" he asked the clerk.

"Twenty dollars," said the clerk. "It's on sale. The wheel is extra."

Behind Jeff was a big, empty aquarium. "Could you keep mice in an aquarium?" he asked the clerk.

"Sure," the clerk said. "But you'll need a piece of wire mesh over the top. You don't want wild mice to get in, or a cat. You'll need some wood shavings for the bottom. And it's best to have a proper water bottle. You don't want the cage to get wet."

"How much is all that?" asked Jeff.

The clerk added things up. Jeff frowned.

"A cage would be cheaper," Dad said.

"I know," said Jeff. He thought about Tilly's Mouse Town. "But the mice would be happier in a bigger place," he said.

"It will take all the money you've saved, Jeff," Dad said. "You'll have to forget your airplane for a long time. You'd better think carefully before you decide."

Jeff thought about Tilly Perkins and her wild bears. He thought about the dragon. He

thought about Bruno and Poppy and Sally sneering at her stories.

What if Tilly Perkins didn't bring the mice? Poppy and Sally would sneer at him, too. Bruno would laugh.

Tilly Perkins doesn't mind being laughed at, but I do, thought Jeff. Then he remembered Tilly Perkins's bright, twinkly eyes. He remembered her journal. And her castle. And her Mouse Town.

"I'll take the aquarium and the other stuff," he said. "Tilly Perkins is worth it."

Next day at school Tilly ran up to him. "Jeff, did you get a mouse cage yet?" she asked.

"I got an aquarium," said Jeff. "That's better."

Bruno hooted. Poppy snorted. Sally sniggered.

Jeff hoped Tilly Perkins would bring the mice. He wasn't at all sure she would. Maybe it would rain on his birthday. He almost hoped so. Then he couldn't have his party. There wasn't room for twenty-four kids in the house.

The day of the birthday party came. The sun

woke Jeff up. When he saw the sun he felt excited. A birthday was a special day. Things would work out.

Everybody was supposed to meet at the park. Jeff and his mom and dad went early to get things ready. They loaded up the car.

"What about the aquarium?" Jeff asked.

"We don't have to take it," Dad said. "It might get broken. Tilly will have to bring the mice in a box. We can bring them home in that."

Jeff could hardly believe his good luck. Now he could say he'd pretended the aquarium if it turned out that Tilly was only pretending the mice. Then the other kids couldn't make fun of him.

He helped his mom and dad set out the food on picnic tables. They lit the fires, so that the kids could roast their hot dogs.

Bruno came first. He always came first to a party. More kids arrived. Poppy and Sally came together. Sally's mother drove them. Nick and Alex came with their dad.

Everybody gave Jeff their gifts. "Happy

birthday," they said.

"Thanks," said Jeff. He piled the gifts under the table. He would open them later.

Tilly did not come. Jeff kept looking out for her. Part of him didn't want her to come. Part did.

"I guess we'll start the picnic," Mom said. "Maybe Tilly isn't coming."

A pickup truck drove into the parking lot. It made a noise like firecrackers. Tilly hopped out.

"Look who's here," said Poppy.

Chapter 8

Jeff's Birthday

Everybody stopped roasting their hot dogs. They stared at Tilly. She wore a blue dress with a skirt that stuck out. It had pink rosebuds printed on it, and a wide pink sash. She had a shiny pink bow in her hair. She wore pink tights. They twisted around her skinny legs. She had shiny black shoes.

"Jeff, why didn't you tell us this was a dress-up party?" Sally said. "I would have worn my party dress."

"My mom wouldn't let me wear mine," Poppy said.

Tilly ran across the grass to Jeff. Her eyes were shining. "Happy birthday, Jeff," she cried. She said it as if she really meant it.

Bruno stood beside Jeff. He scowled at Tilly. "Where's your gift?" he asked. "I thought you were bringing white mice."

"I didn't want them to escape in the park," Tilly said. "They'd get lost and die. My mom's coming to pick me up after. She'll bring the mice."

"I bet," said Poppy.

Jeff's mom smiled at Tilly. "That's fine, Tilly," she said. "Have a hot dog. Be careful. Don't spoil your pretty dress."

"You should have worn jeans like everybody else," Poppy said. "Didn't you know this was a picnic?"

Was Tilly Perkins flustered?

Was Tilly Perkins flabbergasted?

No, she was not. Tilly Perkins smiled at Jeff. "I think people should always dress up for parties," she said. "Even if it is a picnic."

Jeff smiled back at Tilly. She had dressed up

for his party. She made him feel that it was a really special day. Tilly Perkins does what she likes, thought Jeff, not what other people like.

"I know how you feel, Tilly," Dad said. "In the old days ladies used to wear their prettiest dresses at picnics. They wore large hats with flowers and they carried parasols to protect them from the sun. The men wore dark suits and stiff white shirts."

Poppy looked mad. "My mom wouldn't let me wear my best dress to a picnic," she said.

"My mom would have a stroke," Sally said. "How can anybody run races and play baseball dressed like that?"

"Maybe Tilly doesn't want to play," Jeff's mom said. "That's okay."

But after the picnic Tilly ran in all the races. She took off her shiny shoes and won the first race. In the next race Tilly's hair ribbon fell off. She hung it over a branch.

"Tilly, can I borrow your ribbon?" Poppy asked. "My hair keeps falling in my eyes."

"Sure," said Tilly.

Poppy tied back her hair with the ribbon. Jeff could tell Poppy thought she looked pretty.

In the next race Tilly's sash came undone, but Tilly won anyway. She hung her sash over another branch.

Sally borrowed the sash, without even asking. She tied it across her shoulder. "The Queen wears a sash like this," she said.

Tilly Perkins didn't mind. Tilly Perkins is a generous girl, thought Jeff. Even if she didn't bring a gift.

After a few more races they decided to play baseball. Since it was Jeff's birthday, he got to choose his own team. He chose Tilly first. Bruno scowled. Jeff chose Bruno next.

Tilly scored a home run. All the kids on her team cheered, even Bruno.

Jeff was happy. The kids were getting to like Tilly Perkins.

The feet of Tilly's tights wore into holes. After the game she folded the torn bits under her feet and put her shoes back on.

Jeff's mom brought out the birthday cake.

Everyone sang "Happy Birthday." Tilly sang loudest of all. Jeff blew out the candles in one blow. He made a secret wish: "I wish the other kids would really like Tilly." Then he opened his gifts.

"Open mine first," Bruno said.

"No, mine," said Poppy.

Jeff took a long time with each one. He hoped that if he took long enough, the other kids might forget about Tilly's gift.

Nick and Alex brought an exercise wheel for mice, and a ladder for them to climb.

At least they believe Tilly Perkins, thought Jeff.

"Maybe you could exchange those things for something else," said Poppy.

"I don't want to," said Jeff. He smiled at Nick and Alex.

The moms and dads started to arrive. They came to pick up their children. Everyone stood around waiting for Jeff to finish opening his gifts.

"Where's your mom?" Bruno asked Tilly.

"You said she was bringing the mice."

"Maybe the truck broke down," Tilly said cheerfully. "It's always breaking down."

Bruno looked scornful. "That's your story," he said.

The parents wanted to go home. "Come along," they called. "The party's over. Time to go."

"It's not nice to come to a party without a gift," Poppy said. "Here's your dumb ribbon." She snatched it off her hair and threw it at Tilly.

"And here's your sash," Sally said. "My mom would never let me keep mice. She says they're dirty."

"Tilly Perkins broke her promise," Bruno said.

Did Tilly Perkins look wistful?

Did Tilly Perkins look woebegone?

Yes, she did. A little. "Jeff, did you bring the cage for the mice?" she asked.

Poppy smirked. So did Sally.

Bruno sneered. "No, he didn't," he said.

"Jeff's not dumb."

Jeff hesitated. He *could* say he'd taken the aquarium back to the pet shop. He *could* say he'd never bought one in the first place. He *could* say he'd only been pretending, like Tilly. Tilly waited.

"No," said Jeff. "I didn't bring it. My dad thought it might break. We left it at home. It's all ready for the mice." His face felt hot. He wondered why. Tilly Perkins was the one whose face should be red.

"You wasted your money," Sally said.

"Don't say we didn't warn you," said Poppy.

"Dummy. I told you she wouldn't bring any mice," said Bruno.

"She doesn't have to," said Jeff. "We can pretend about the mice."

Tilly Perkins looked cheerful again. She tipped her head to one side. "Jeff, on Monday will you play with me at recess?"

"If you play with *her*, you can't play with me, ever," said Bruno.

Jeff thought about that.

"And I'll never talk to you again, Jeff Brown," said Poppy.

"I won't either," said Sally.

Jeff thought about that too. None of the other kids, except the twins, would play with him.

Did Jeff whimper?

Did Jeff whine?

No, he did not. He lifted his chin. "So what!" he said loudly. "Yes, Tilly Perkins, I'll play with you every day at recess. I want to be your friend."

"Even though I didn't bring the mice?"

"Yes," Jeff said.

Tilly's eyes twinkled as if she knew a secret.

Chapter 9

Tilly's Gift

Most of the kids had left with their parents.

"Don't worry, Tilly," Jeff's mom said. "We'll drive you home."

Just then a truck bounced into the parking lot with a sound like firecrackers exploding.

"Here's my mom," Tilly cried. She ran across the grass to the truck and hopped in.

Jeff watched. So did Bruno. He was always the last to leave a party. Poppy and Sally watched too.

"Tilly Perkins didn't even say thank you," Poppy said.

"She didn't even say goodbye," said Sally.

"She doesn't have to," Jeff said. He really didn't mind that Tilly had not said thank you. But he felt hurt that she hadn't said goodbye.

The truck didn't move. After a while Tilly Perkins climbed out of the truck again. She came out backwards. Slowly she turned around. She had a box in her hands. Tilly walked across the grass, heel and toe, heel and toe, like someone in an egg and spoon race. She held the box very carefully.

Jeff held his breath. Did Tilly Perkins have his mice? Real, live mice? Or was she just pretending? He ran to meet her.

"Wait till we get to the picnic table," Tilly Perkins said.

A woman got out of the driver's side of the truck. She was dressed in crumpled pants and a baggy sweater. She followed Tilly and Jeff across to the picnic table.

"Hi," she said, "I'm Nora Perkins, Tilly's mom. Sorry I'm late. I had a hard time rounding up the mice." She laughed a merry laugh.

Perhaps the laugh meant that the mice were not real. Perhaps it meant that Tilly and her mother were joking.

"We ran races," Poppy said. "Tilly ruined her tights."

"That's all right," Nora Perkins said. She spoke slowly, as if she had lots of time. "We'll chop them off and sew up the ends. Then we'll start again. Tilly doesn't like to wear jeans. Do you, Princess?"

Tilly's mother did not sound like Poppy's mother, or Sally's. She sounded a lot nicer.

Tilly put the box on the table. She opened up the top, just a little bit. "Can you see them?" she whispered.

Jeff peeped inside. At first all he could see was a pile of wood shavings. Then he spied two petal-shaped ears. Then two bright black eyes. Then some trembling white whiskers and a tiny pink nose. Then a second white head popped out of the straw.

"Do you like them?" Tilly Perkins asked.

Jeff liked them so much he couldn't speak. He

couldn't even say thank you.

Did Tilly Perkins get sulky?

Did Tilly Perkins get sore?

No, she did not. Tilly Perkins understood. "They'll run up your arm," she said. "And down the other. And look for sunflower seeds in your pocket. They're very tame."

"Oooooh," squealed Poppy. "Gross."

"Eeeeh," squeaked Sally. "Creepy."

"Let me see," Bruno cried. He pushed his head in beside Jeff's.

Then Poppy and Sally wanted a turn looking in the box.

"They're kind of cute," said Poppy.

"Look at their little pink noses," said Sally.

"Can he keep them?" Nora Perkins asked Jeff's mom and dad. "Tilly said it was all right, but I thought I'd better check."

"It's all right," Jeff's dad said. "But he has to look after them."

"And keep them in his own room," Jeff's mom added.

"You should put cardboard tubes in the

cage," Tilly said. "Use the ones out of paper towels and toilet rolls. The mice like to run through tunnels. You can build them some stairs and bridges. You can make buildings out of old shoe boxes. I keep my Mouse Town next to my dragon's castle. I've got lots of mice. I'll give you some more if you like."

"Is that true, Tilly Perkins?" Poppy asked. "Do you *really* have a Mouse Town?"

"Sure," said Tilly Perkins.

"Why don't you ever write about Mouse Town in your journal?" Sally asked.

"I do," Tilly Perkins said. "I write about it a whole bunch. It's just that I never read out about it."

"Jeff can come to visit the farm sometime," Nora Perkins said. "We have lots of animals."

"Wild animals?" Bruno asked.

Nora Perkins's laugh sounded like bubbles bursting. "They're a wild lot all right."

Nobody was sure if that meant yes or no.

"Say, Tilly," Bruno said. "If you have too many mice, I could take some off your hands."

"I'm going to ask my mother if I can have some," Poppy said.

"Me too," said Sally. "We have to go now. My mom's waiting in the car. Goodbye Jeff. Thanks for the party."

"Thanks for the party," Poppy said. "See you at school on Monday. Goodbye, Tilly Perkins."

As usual, Bruno was the last to leave. Tilly and her mother drove away in their firecracker truck. Bruno and Jeff waved goodbye. Tilly leaned out of the window and waved her sash.

"Bruno, I never said I have *too many* mice," she called out from the truck. "When's your birthday?"

"Next month," Bruno said.

"By then I might have some baby dragons," Tilly Perkins shouted as the truck drove away.

"Tilly Perkins doesn't really have a dragon, does she?" Bruno asked Jeff.

Jeff thought about the iguana. He smiled. "Could be," he said. "With Tilly Perkins, you just never know."

Brenda Bellingham was born in Liverpool,
England, and now makes her home in Alberta.
She has two children, both grown up, and a cat
named Mao, who may or may not be grown up
— he won't tell his age to anyone.

Brenda has published three other books with
Scholastic: *The Curse of the Silver Box, Two
Parents Too Many* and *Dragons Don't Read Books*,
as well as *Joanie's Magic Boots* (Tree Frog Press)
and *Storm Child* (Lorimer). She is working on
several new projects including some more
stories about Tilly and Jeff. When she is not
writing, she teaches courses and visits schools,
reads or knits.